# Tom's Sausage Lion

**Michael Morpurgo**
**Illustrated by Robina Green**

**A & C Black · London**

**The Comets Series**
Series Editor, Amy Gibbs

| | |
|---|---|
| **King Fernando** | John Bartholomew |
| **A Witch in Time** | Terry Deary |
| **Tom's Sausage Lion** | Michael Morpurgo |
| **Odin's Monster** | Susan Price |
| **The Air-Raid Shelter** | Jeremy Strong |

*For Kay, Hussein, Hannan and Adam*

Morpurgo, Michael
Tom's sausage lion.—(Comets)
I. Title  II. Series
823'.914[J]  PZ7

ISBN 0-7136-2757-3

Published by A & C Black (Publishers) Limited
35 Bedford Row, London WC1R 4JH

Text © 1986 Michael Morpurgo
Illustrations © 1986 Robina Green

First published 1986

ISBN 0-7136-2757-3

Filmset by August Filmsetting, Haydock, St. Helens
Printed in Great Britain by R J Acford Ltd., Chichester, Sussex

## Chapter One

It was Christmas Eve when Tom first saw the lion. His mother had sent him out to fetch the logs, and there was a lion padding through the orchard with a string of sausages hanging from its mouth. Tom ran back inside the house to tell them, but his father just laughed and his mother said he must have been imagining things. He told them and he told them, but they wouldn't even come out to look.

'But it's true,' Tom shouted. 'It was a real lion, I know it was.'

'Perhaps it just looked like a lion,' said his mother. 'After all it is getting dark outside, isn't it dear?'

'It couldn't have been anything else,' Tom said. 'There's nothing else looks like a lion.' But they wouldn't listen.

'That's enough, Tom,' said his father who was already cross. 'It's Christmas Eve, not April Fool's Day. You don't really expect us to believe a story like that do you? We're not that stupid you know. I don't want to hear another word about it, hear me? Else I'll send you to your room, Christmas Eve or no Christmas Eve.'

'But it was a lion, a real lion,' said Tom. 'Honest.'

'Right, that's it,' his father said banging the table and pointing to the door. 'Upstairs.'

And so Tom was sent to bed early on Christmas Eve and when he dreamt that night it was not of angels or of Father Christmas, but of lions.

All Christmas Day nothing more was said about the lion, until Uncle Bertie and Aunty Rose came for tea as they always did. Even then Tom didn't really mean to tell them about the lion, because he knew they wouldn't believe him either. Somehow it just slipped out.

'And what's the little lad going to be when he grows up?' Uncle Bertie asked, putting his teacup down. 'Is he going to be a farmer like his Dad?'

'My, hasn't he grown again!' said Aunty Rose. 'Nine years old and nearly as tall as his Mum. Spitting image of his father though. Same ginger hair and rosy cheeks. Break the girls' hearts he will. Just like his Dad,' and she stuffed another mince pie into her mouth.

That's her fifth mince pie, Tom thought. She'll burst if she eats any more. They always ask me so many questions and they always talk about me as if I'm not there. And I have to kiss Aunty Rose when they come and when they go. I wouldn't mind, but she squeezes me so tight and she always leaves lipstick on my face.

'Train driver last year, wasn't it?' Uncle Bertie said. 'Didn't he want to be a train driver?'

'Lorry driver,' said Tom. 'But I've changed my mind. I want to be a lion-tamer now.' It was the first thing that came into his head.

'A what?' Aunty Rose laughed, and she patted her chest to stop herself choking on the mince pie she had just swallowed. 'What do you want to do that for?'

''Cos I like lions,' Tom said.

'You ever seen one?' Uncle Bertie asked.

'Yesterday,' said Tom. 'Saw one yesterday.' And Tom felt his mother and father glaring at him.

'Went to the zoo did you dear?' Aunty Rose said and sipped her tea, her little finger cocked in the air. Tom shook his head. 'Circus was it then?'

'No,' said Tom.

'Television? You saw it on the telly then?' Aunty Rose went on. Tom shook his head again.

'I saw a real one,' he said.

'That's enough, Tom,' said his father gruffly. 'No more of your stories now. Aunty Rose isn't interested.'

'Wasn't a story, Dad,' Tom said. 'It's the honest truth, like I told you.'

'We said we weren't going to talk about it any more, didn't we dear,' said his mother, putting a hand on his arm.

'But I saw it,' said Tom. 'I know I did. I'm not

5

making it up. It was a lion. I know it was. You just won't believe me, that's all.' Tears of anger came into his eyes.

'I believe you saw something, Tom dear,' said his mother. 'But it couldn't have been a lion, could it, because they're all in zoos or circuses. You don't find them just wandering around the place.'

Aunty Rose looked around her like a flustered hen. 'What are you all talking about?' she asked.

'What they're talking about, Rose,' said Tom's father, 'is a lot of old nonsense. That's what it is. Tom comes running in here yesterday evening screaming his head off. "I've seen a lion," he says, "Walking through the orchard, just behind Mrs Blunden's cottage"—a lion with a string of sausages hanging out of his mouth, if you please. Believe that, you believe anything.' And he turned angrily to Tom. 'Now I don't want to hear any more about it, Tom.'

The phone rang in the kitchen and Tom's mother left the room to answer it. Tom tried to blink back his tears and almost succeeded except for one large tear that trickled down his cheek and dropped on to his plate.

'Now look what you've done,' said Aunty Rose. 'You've gone and upset him.' She pulled her handkerchief out of her sleeve and wiped Tom's face. 'We can't have tears on Christmas Day, can we now?

We all make mistakes from time to time. It's nothing to cry about.' She planted a noisy kiss on his ear just as his mother came back into the room.

'Who was it?' his father asked.

'It's all very strange,' she said. 'That was Mrs Blunden on the phone.' Tom looked up.

'What did she want?' Tom's father asked. 'The pigs haven't got into her garden again, have they?'

'No,' she said. 'She just wanted to know if the butcher had delivered some of her meat to us by mistake yesterday. If she's out he usually leaves her meat in the box by her gate. Well some of it was there when she came back yesterday evening but not all of it and she wondered if we had it.'

'It was sausages, wasn't it?' Tom said.

'Yes,' she said. 'three pounds of pork sausages, and they've gone.'

'See? I told you, didn't I?' said Tom. 'I wasn't making it up, was I?'

For a moment there was a silence around the table and then his father spoke up. 'Just because Mrs Blunden's sausages have gone missing, that doesn't mean a lion took them, does it? Could have been anything, couldn't it? Fox, cat, badger, dog? Could have been that sheepdog of yours, that Sam. He's always up to some mischief or other. Needs a good hiding that one. Not trained like he should be.'

'It wasn't Sam, Dad.' said Tom. 'He was too big

to be Sam. Long as this table he was, Dad, honest. Face like a cat with whiskers and pricked up pointed ears. Great long tail he had. I saw him, Dad, close as I am to you. The sausages were dragging along the ground so's he was treading on them. Sort of gingery light brown he was.'

'Sam's a sandy sort of a colour, isn't he, dear?' Tom's mother said. 'It could have been him, couldn't it? Perhaps it was a bit dark to see properly. And you know Sam's a terrible thief. He's had sausages off our kitchen table before now, Tom, remember?'

'S'pose so,' said Tom. 'But . . . . . . . .'

'No buts, Tom,' said his father firmly. 'Now you go and make sure that dog of yours is shut up for the night. He'll be turning over the dustbins again else. He's always at the dustbins that dog.' Tom got up. 'And whilst you're at it, you can shut up the hens and the geese as well.'

Tom was glad to leave. He was just closing the door behind him when he heard Uncle Bertie call out, 'Better shut 'em up, lad, just in case there's lions about.'

'Or elephants,' said Aunty Rose. And they all howled with laughter. Come to think of it, Tom thought, Aunty Rose looks a bit like an elephant. Give her nose a pull and you couldn't tell the difference. It made him happy to think of that as he put on his boots by the back door.

8

He had one boot half on when he heard the dustbin lid clattering to the ground outside. 'Sam,' he called. 'Get out of it,' and he opened the door and peered out into the darkness. By this time he had his other boot on. He groped for the outside light switch and turned it on. The lion stood about six feet away from him. Tom was too surprised even to be frightened. The remains of the Christmas turkey were at the lion's feet and there were brussels sprout leaves caught in his whiskers. He licked his lips once as he looked at Tom and then sat down by the turkey bones and began to crunch them. He had very big white teeth.

Tom shut the door again and raced back across the kitchen to the sitting room. They were still laughing.

'It's him, it's him! He's outside,' Tom said. 'Quick!'

'Who is?' his father asked.

9

'Your lion I suppose,' said Uncle Bertie, and he began to shake with laughter.

'Yes,' said Tom as calmly as he could. 'It's my lion and he's outside now eating the turkey you put out in the dustbin, Mum.' The faces around him had all turned serious. 'Come and look,' he said. 'Quick, he's outside the back door.'

'If you're joking . . . . . .' said his father.

'I'm not,' Tom said. 'Honest I'm not. Come quick else he'll be gone. And you mustn't make a noise else you'll frighten him away.'

In their paper hats they stole through the kitchen towards the back door. His father took down the gun from the shelf, slipped in two cartridges and snapped it shut. He opened the door but only just wide enough so that he could put his head round.

'See, Dad, I told you, didn't I? It's a lion, isn't it? He won't hurt you,' said Tom. 'He's just hungry, that's all.'

'Some lion,' his father said, and threw open the door. 'Why don't you have another look, Tom?' Tom's heart sank. He looked outside the door. All he could see of Sam at first was his wagging tail. The rest of him was inside the dustbin. When he did turn round there was a sausage in his mouth.

'So that's your lion is it?' said Uncle Bertie, and he began to laugh again. 'So that's Tom's sausage lion.'

## Chapter Two

Only one thing mattered to Tom now. He had to prove to his mother and father that he had not been making it all up. And there was only one way to do that. He had to find the lion, and bring him home. He had no idea how he was going to do it, but he had to try.

So every day for the rest of the holidays Tom searched the farm and the high moor beyond for some trace of the lion. He took Sam with him, hoping he would be able to pick up the scent and follow it. Sam found plenty of rabbits and hares and pheasants, and he chased them all over the moor, but he could find no lion. There were no footprints to follow either because the ground was bone-hard with frost. Even the puddles were frozen over.

His mother and father were too busy lambing the sheep to bother where he was. So long as he came back on time for meals, they asked no questions. By the time he went back to school they had quite forgotten about Tom's sausage lion. Tom knew it was no good trying to make them believe him any more. They would never believe him now, not until they saw the lion for themselves.

Tom was very happy to go back to school that term. Upcott Farm where he lived was over three miles from town, so that he hardly ever saw his school friends in the holidays. At home there was only Sam to talk to about his lion and Tom was never really sure whether Sam believed him or not.

When he got on the school bus that first morning he was longing to tell someone about his lion. He hardly waited till he sat down before he told them the whole story.

'Twice I seen him,' he said. 'Once with Mrs Blunden's sausages and once with the turkey. Massive he was. Got green eyes, at least I think they were green. And you should've seen his teeth—long as my fingers they were. He crunched those turkey bones just like they were wafers.' When he had finished he looked around at his friends. They were all open-mouthed. None of them said anything until Barry Parsons spoke up. Barry Parsons had never liked Tom, and Tom had never much liked him. Tom had taken his place as right back in the school football team and Barry had never forgiven him.

'Pull the other one, Tom,' said Barry. 'Aren't no lions around here.'

'Well I seen him,' Tom said, looking around at the others. He could see they didn't believe him either. 'It's true. I did.'

'Who else saw it then?' Barry asked.

'Just me,' Tom said quietly. 'Wasn't anyone else there. But I saw him right close up. Honest.'

'Then why didn't he eat you if you were that close?' Barry went on. 'S'pose you shook his paw and wished him happy Christmas.' And then the others began to laugh. Barry left his seat and went down on all fours in the gangway and crawled up and down the bus roaring like a lion, clawing at everyone and shouting out: 'Got any sausages? I'm Tom's lion. Got any turkey? I'm Tom's lion.' And the whole bus howled with laughter. Tom turned his face to the window so they couldn't see how angry he was. He just could not understand why no one would believe him. Even his best friends were laughing at him. Well he'd show them. He'd show them all.

Mr Morgan was Tom's class teacher. He was funny when he was in a good mood, and horrible when he was not. And this morning Mr Morgan was not in a good mood. He told them so as soon as he came into the classroom. 'Some idiot skidded into my car on the way to school this morning, so I'm not a happy man. Understand?'

'Yes, Sir,' they chorused.

'It's your job to make me happy, isn't it?'

'Yes, Sir.'

'So I want each of you to tell me the best thing, the funniest thing, or the most exciting thing that's happened to you during the holidays.' He came to Tom's desk and looked down at him.

'And what's the matter with you, Tom Goss? You look down in the mouth this morning. I recognise a fellow sufferer. You're usually a cheerful sort of Charlie, Tom. First day of term, is that what it is?'

'Yes, Sir,' said Tom.

'Same for all of us,' Mr Morgan sighed and shook his head. 'Still, we mustn't feel sorry for ourselves, must we? We'll start with you, Tom. Stand up then. Don't be shy.'

Tom stood up. He couldn't think of anything to say. Everyone was looking at him, waiting.

'Come on Tom,' said Mr Morgan. 'What about Christmas Day? Something good must have happened on Christmas Day surely? Did you get any nice presents?'

'He got a lion,' said Barry, and the whole class broke into giggles.

'Oh dear, oh dear,' said Mr Morgan, advancing towards Barry's desk and silencing the class as he went. 'Oh dear, oh dear. Barry the Clown is back. But he's come to the wrong place hasn't he? This isn't a circus, boy. No, it's my class, see? And when I ask for you to speak, you'll speak. Until then put a sock in it—there's a good boy, else I'll get ugly. And you don't want me ugly, do you?'

'No Sir,' said Barry.

'Good. Now Tom, what's all this about a lion?'

Tom looked at Mr Morgan. Like all the children, he had always been a little frightened of him. Everyone knew he had a wicked temper. But he had no choice anyway, not now. He couldn't get out of it. 'Saw him on Christmas Eve first,' Tom said. 'In the orchard it was.'

'What? A lion? A real live lion?' Mr Morgan said. Tom nodded and there were one or two sniggers around him, swiftly silenced by a glance from Mr Morgan.

'Go on boy, I'm listening.'

'Well, Sir. He was walking through the apple trees with Mrs Blunden's sausages hanging out of his mouth, and when he saw me, he just ran off.

Almost tripped over them, he did.'

'Tripped over what?' Mr Morgan asked.

'The sausages, Sir.' Tom said. 'Then I saw him again the next day, just after tea on Christmas Day. He was just outside the back door, Sir, helping himself to the turkey bones Mum had put out in the dustbin, and he saw me too. I saw him clear as day.'

'Ah, but I thought you said it was after tea,' said Mr Morgan, 'so it would be getting dark, wouldn't it?'

'Had the outside light on, Sir.' Tom said. 'It was a lion, honest it was Sir, just like I seen in books and on the telly.'

Mr Morgan thought for a moment, and then his face broke into a smile. 'That's what I like, Tom, a boy with a bit of imagination. It's a good story. Only one thing wrong with it. If this lion saw you why didn't he attack you? I mean you're a fairly tasty morsel for a hungry lion I'd have thought.' And everyone was laughing openly now.

'But it's all true, Sir.' Tom shouted. 'It's not a story. It's true, every word of it.'

Mr Morgan's smile vanished. 'Take care boy. I won't be shouted at and I won't be lied to.'

'It's not a lie, Sir.' Tom said.

'Then who else saw it?' Mr Morgan said. 'You must have called someone when you saw it outside the back door.'

'No one else saw it.' Barry interrupted.

'Silence!' Mr Morgan bellowed, and he turned back to Tom. 'So you found a lion outside your back door and you never called anyone?'

'Yes, Sir. I did, Sir. I called my Mum and Dad. And Uncle Bertie and Aunty Rose were there too. They came.'

'So they saw it too then?'

'No, not exactly,' Tom said.

'What do you mean, "not exactly"?'

'Well, by the time they got there, it had run off and Sam was there instead.'

'Sam?'

'My dog, Sir. But the lion was there, Sir, I know he was. Honest, Sir.'

'Honest? Honest? You don't know the meaning of the word,' Mr Morgan thundered. 'Do you expect me to believe you saw a real live lion running around with a string of sausages, and helping himself to your Christmas turkey? Now either you're lying to me, Tom, or you had too much cider at Christmas, and you were seeing things that weren't there. Boys your age shouldn't be drinking cider.'

'I don't like cider, Sir,' said Tom defiantly. 'And I'm not lying.' All fear of Mr Morgan now left him. He felt suddenly quite alone in the world, and stronger for it. 'I saw that lion,' he said, looking Mr Morgan straight in the eye.

Mr Morgan gave him every punishment there was. He was sent to Miss Colvin, the Headmistress, where he was questioned for over twenty minutes. She didn't believe him either. She said she was disappointed in him, and that liars often ended up in trouble or even in prison when they grew up. In break he had to write out 'I must not lie' one hundred times, and he spent the rest of the morning standing with his face to the corner.

By the lunch-break everyone in the school knew the story of Tom's sausage lion, and even some of the little infants came up and growled at him in the cloakroom when he was putting on his coat and scarf. They clawed at his back and then ran off shrieking when he turned round.

Clare Newman was standing by the door. She was the butcher's daughter and she was the cleverest girl in Tom's class. She always had her head in some book or other. She was tiny, tiny enough to be an infant and she wore great thick glasses that she was always losing or breaking. There always seemed to be a piece of elastoplast holding them together. She had an open book in her hand.

'Was it this one?' she asked, walking over to him. 'Was it the same as this one?' Tom thought for a moment she was teasing him, but then he remembered that Clare Newman was not like that. He looked down at the book. 'The cougar, puma or mountain lion,' he read out loud. And there was a picture of the same kind of lion he had seen in the orchard on Christmas Eve.

'That's him, that's just like him,' Tom said. 'But how'd you know?'

''Cos I seen him just like you did, that's why,' said Clare. 'I was on the rounds with my Dad, Christmas Eve it was. Dad was delivering Mrs Blunden's meat and I was waiting for him in the van. I looked up and there he was looking through the window at me. We just looked at each other for a moment and then he ran off.'

'Didn't you tell your Dad?' Tom asked.

'Course I did, but he didn't believe me. I could hardly believe it myself, not till I heard you telling Mr Morgan. See, I'd left my glasses at home. I'm always forgetting them and I'm as blind as a bat without my glasses—everyone knows that. Can't see a sausage without them.'

'That meant to be funny, is it?' Tom said.

'No,' Clare said, and she laughed. 'It wasn't meant to be; but come to think of it, it was quite funny, wasn't it?'

Tom smiled for the first time that day. 'I'm glad you believe me,' he said. 'I was beginning to think I was imagining things.'

'Well we weren't, were we?' said Clare.

## Chapter Three

'P'raps if we told the Police,' Clare said. 'P'raps they'd believe us. We got to make someone believe us before he gets hungry.'

'What d'you mean?' Tom said.

'Well, once he gets hungry and there's no more sausages to steal or dustbins to rob, then he'll have to kill. Got to eat, hasn't he? Listen to this.' She opened her book again. 'When it hunts,' she read out, 'it shows a daring skill and cruelty equal to that of a tiger. One is reported to have killed fifty sheep in a single night.'

'Do they kill people as well?' Tom said.

Clare shook her head. 'Hardly ever—that's what my book says anyway. Only when they're very hungry.'

The Police Station was just five minutes down the road from the school. They could be back by the end of playtime. They sneaked out of the school gates while Mr Morgan's back was turned and ran all the way there.

The policeman looked down at the two breathless children, and tapped his pencil on the counter. 'Lost something, have you?' he asked.

'No,' said Tom. 'We seen something.'

The policeman sounded bored. 'Oh yes, and what have you seen then? Flying saucers is it, or is it pink elephants p'raps?' and he snorted with laughter.

'A lion,' said Tom. 'I seen a lion running off with Mrs Blunden's sausages and she's seen it too, haven't you?'

Clare nodded. 'Close as I am to you,' she said.

'Now let me get this clear. You've seen a lion have you, running off with Mrs Blunden's sausages, it that it?'

'Yes,' said Tom and Clare together.

'And what colour was this lion?' said the Policeman, leaning forward on his elbows, and smiling at them. 'Purple was he, with green spots?'

'It was a puma,' said Clare. 'A mountain lion. It's in my book. They come from America. Sort of tawny yellow colour they are.'

'So this lion swam here all the way across from America has it?' The smile left his face. 'What do you think I am? I wasn't born yesterday you know. Now you get along out of here and stop wasting my time. Lions indeed. Whatever next? Get off with you before I call the Sergeant.'

They walked back to school in silence and slipped into the playground without being noticed. Playtime was still on. 'I've been thinking,' said Clare, sitting down by the railings. 'You could search that moor forever and never find him, couldn't you?'

'S'pose so,' Tom said.

'So we've got to tempt him back, haven't we?'

'How?' Tom asked.

'Food,' Clare said, taking off her glasses and cleaning them with her skirt. 'That's what he came for in the first place, wasn't it? He wouldn't have risked coming near your house if he wasn't hungry. So why don't we put out some meat for him to tempt him back? You could keep a lookout and photograph him when he comes. If they saw a photo they'd have to believe us then, wouldn't they? Got a camera, have you?'

Tom shook his head, 'No,' he said.

'Well I have,' she said. 'And it's got a flash on it too. You can borrow it.'

'And where'd we get the food from?' Tom asked.

'My Dad's a butcher, remember?' Clare said, and breathed on her glasses. 'I'll bring some into school tomorrow. All right?'

'Got a new girlfriend, have we Tarzan?' It was Barry. 'You Tarzan, she Jane, is that it?' Tom was surrounded by grinning faces. Barry began to growl at him like a lion and then everyone copied him. Something snapped suddenly inside Tom. He had had enough. He threw himself at Barry, kicking and punching until they ended up rolling on the ground together.

Mr Morgan broke through the crowd of chanting children and pulled them apart before any real damage was done. But Tom was glad to see that he had given Barry a bloody nose.

'So it's fighting now, is it Tom Goss?' Mr Morgan said. 'Quite the little lionheart aren't we? What's the matter with you boy? Never seen you fighting like this before. Haven't you been in enough trouble today without this? Now get inside the two of you. Tom you can clean out the guinea-pigs and wipe down the blackboard. Barry, you can sweep the classroom, and tidy the bookshelves. Off you go. Any more of this and I'll bang your heads together, hear me?'

No one dared say a word about Tom's sausage lion after his fight with Barry. There were no more mocking growls, and Tom was feeling a lot happier when he got off the bus and ran up the lane towards home. Sam usually ran out to meet him, but he wasn't there today. 'Where's Sam?' he said as he came through into the kitchen. His mother and father were sitting at the table. Father still had his boots on and he looked grim.

'Good day dear?' Tom's mother said as usual, standing up and wiping her hands on her apron. 'Take your coat off and I'll get you your tea.'

'Where's Sam?' said Tom, who could tell from their faces something was being hidden from him.

'Gone,' said his father, 'And if he knows what's good for him, he'll stay away too.'

'What's happened?' said Tom, half out of his coat. 'What's the matter? What d'you mean Sam's gone? Gone where?'

'I don't know and I don't care.' said his father. And he looked up at Tom. 'I warned you and I warned you. I told you to keep that dog of yours shut up didn't I? I told you he was getting out of control.'

'It's not Tom's fault, dear,' said Tom's mother. 'These things happen. We've lost lambs before.'

'But these weren't just lost, were they?' his father said, banging the table. 'That dog of his killed them.'

'Sam?' said Tom. 'Sam killed some sheep. He couldn't have. How d'you know that it was him?'

'Because I saw him. I saw him running away and

that's good enough for me. Just after lunch it was. First thing I saw was the sheep bolting across the hill on the other side of the brook. I thought it was a fox at first, so I came in here and got my gun. By the time I got out there again there was that dog of yours with three lambs lying beside him on the ground. The shot frightened him and he took off up into the woods going like a train.'

'You shot at Sam? You shot at him?' Tom shouted.

'Course I did,' his father said. 'What'd you expect me to do? Stand there and watch him killing my sheep? I had to frighten him off somehow. Don't worry. I didn't hit him. I was too far away and I was aiming above his head anyway. But as soon as he comes back that dog'll have to go. You can't have a dog on a farm that kills sheep.'

'You mean you'll have him put to sleep?' Tom said. 'But you can't, you can't. It wasn't him that killed those sheep, it couldn't have been. Sam's not a sheep killer. He's been around sheep all his life. He wouldn't kill them. It was the lion, it must've been.'

'That was no lion I saw out there this afternoon, Tom. It was Sam. He killed those sheep and when he comes back he'll have to go—that's all there is to it.'

'It's not fair,' said Tom, trying not to cry. 'It's not fair. Sam didn't do it. I know he didn't. And what's more I'll prove it.' And he shrugged on his coat again and ran out of the door.

His mother called after him to come back, but he ignored her. He ran down across the meadow behind the house and jumped the stream at the bottom. There were no sheep left in the field—his father must have brought them in for safety—but halfway up the hill he saw the wool on the ground where the lambs must have been killed. From the wool there was a trail of blood on the grass that lead up to the fence and into the thick oak wood beyond. He stopped at the edge of the wood and called out. 'Sam! Sam!' And he put his fingers into his teeth and whistled. The valley echoed, but there was no answering bark.

He crawled under the fence and made his way into the wood. Every now and then he stopped to call out for Sam, but all he ever heard was the hoot of an owl, and once the cry of a startled pheasant. It was getting dark now but he ran deeper and deeper into the trees until at last he could see the other side of the wood and the open moor beyond. He stood still so he could listen.

'Sam! Sam!' he called out; and suddenly from only a few feet away he heard a rustle of leaves and a faint whimper. He found Sam lying at the foot of a tree. There was a gash on his front leg and one of his paws was covered in blood. He was panting hard, his pink tongue lolling out of his mouth. He looked very tired and weak.

'You all right, Sam?' said Tom kneeling down beside him and stroking his head. 'Where've you been, Sam? What've you been up to? I bet I know how you got that cut. You stood up to that lion, didn't you? Not afraid of anything are you? Not even a lion.' He looked closer at the wound. 'It's not too deep, Sam. You're lucky to be alive, you know that. I can't take you to the vet and I can't take you home either. Just have to look after you myself. If I tell them you were only trying to look after the sheep, just doing your job, they wouldn't believe me. If I tell them you chased away a lion, they wouldn't believe me. See Sam, they think it was you that killed those lambs—that's why Dad fired that shot at you—but I expect you know that already. You're not stupid, are you? I'll have to find some-where secret, somewhere safe for you to stay till they find out it wasn't you that did it.'

He picked Sam up and carried him down to the stream. He sat down beside him and washed the leg until all the blood was gone. Sam kept looking over his shoulder and whining. Tom thought it was the wound that must be hurting him and washed it more gently.

'Got to keep it clean,' he said, sitting back on his heels. 'I've got it. I've got it,' he said. 'There's one place where they'll never find you—Ghost Cottage, that old ruined cottage on the other side of the wood. Father keeps a few tools in there and some hay, but no one ever goes there in winter. You'll be all right, Sam, you'll be all right. As soon as I've found that lion and taken a photo of it; then they'll all know it wasn't you that killed those lambs and you'll be able to come home again. But I've got to find that lion first, haven't I Sam? And he's out there somewhere on the moor, I know he is. You chased him out there, didn't you?'

Tom never looked up into the great oak tree above his head. If he had, he would have seen the mountain lion stretched out along a branch, watching him. He was tired and hungry. He'd never even had time to eat the lambs he'd killed before that dog was on him. He'd tried to fight him off, but the dog was too fierce for him. He'd tried to outrun him but the dog was too quick for him. There was only one thing he could do, climb a tree and hide. He was still hungry but at least he was safe.

## Chapter Four

Sam was lying on the bed of hay which Tom had spread out for him in a corner of the room. The rest of Ghost Cottage was full of hay bales stacked to the the ceiling.

'You've got the whole cottage to yourself,' said Tom. 'There'll be a few mice and rats around, but you like a good rat chase anyway, don't you? You'll be warm enough here, and I'll be back tomorrow with some food after I get back from school. I'll bring some water, too, to wash that cut of yours. And remember, not a bark out of you, not a whimper, you understand?'

Sam seemed to, for his head was on one side, his ears pricked and listening. 'If Dad finds you here you're done for, you know that don't you? Tom crouched down beside Sam and scratched him behind the ears where he liked it. ''Night Sam. Be good. See you tomorrow then.'

The next morning Tom sat by himself in the front of the bus, as far away from everyone as he could. He wondered if Clare Newman had forgotten about the meat and the camera. But he need not have worried. As he got out of the bus she was waiting for him, and they went off together around the back of the bicycle shed so they could talk without being overheard.

'You got it?' he asked, and she smiled and patted her satchel.

'Beef scraps,' she said. 'And I've got my camera too. All in here. Did you see him again?'

'No,' said Tom. 'But he's done what you said he would. He's gone and killed three of my Dad's lambs.' And he told Clare all about Sam and how he'd found him lying hurt in the woods. 'Dad thinks Sam did it and if he finds him he's going to have him put to sleep. But he won't find him 'cos I've hidden him somewhere safe, somewhere they won't find him. But we got to prove it was the lion that did it, Clare. I can't keep Sam hidden forever. We got to find that lion. We got to.'

'He'll come for the meat,' Clare said. 'You'll see. Where are you going to put it?'

'Haven't thought really,' Tom said. 'He was heading off down through the woods towards the moor after he killed the lambs. Sam must have been following him, and that's where I found him, down by the stream. If the lion's been there once, he might come back again I suppose.'

'That's as good a place as any,' Clare said. 'P'raps he'll come back to drink there. He's got to drink. You've got to put the meat right by the stream, somewhere where it's muddy.'

'Why?'

'Footprints,' said Clare. 'You've got to be sure it's him taking the meat, haven't you? I mean it could be a buzzard or a fox or a crow or anything. I looked it up in the book and I done a tracing of a mountain lion's footprint. It's in the camera case.' She checked to see that no one was looking and then took out the bag of meat and the camera and stuffed it down the bottom of Tom's bag.

'Can you bring some more tomorrow?' Tom asked. 'He may not come for it first time.'

'I'll bring some every day until he does,' Clare said. 'Father won't miss it. It's only scraps—goes into sausages anyway. And he likes sausagemeat, doesn't he?' She turned to go. 'I'm glad you gave Barry what for yesterday. I'd have done it myself only I'm a bit small. He's always on about my glasses and about how small I am. G'luck.' And she was gone.

Tom wondered why he had never talked to her much before. Perhaps it was because she was always reading. She's the first girl I've ever really liked, Tom thought.

All day Tom could think of nothing but Sam and the lion. He got two detentions for not paying attention, but he didn't mind. That afternoon as soon as he got off the bus he raced off down across the farm to Ghost Cottage. Sam was waiting by the door as he opened it. He jumped up at him, licking Tom's face and nose and ears until he found something more interesting in Tom's bag.

Tom scooped out a handful of meat scraps and fed them to the dog bit by bit. 'It's not really for you,' he said. 'But she's put plenty in here. The rest's for the lion, Sam. Just got to get one photograph of him and I can take you home again. I want to see their faces, Sam, when they see it really was a lion.'

Sam seemed a lot stronger now, although he was limping on his bad leg. Tom spent as long as he could with Sam, cleaning the cut again and talking to him. Sam whimpered a bit as he left, but when Tom stole back to the window to make sure he was all right, Sam had his nose in the hay bales sniffing out mice and rats, and he seemed quite happy.

'Bit late back aren't you Tom?' said his mother.

'Bus was late.' Tom said and he felt his father look at him sharply.

'Funny,' he said, 'thought I heard it go by the end of the lane some time ago. You been off looking for Sam, haven't you? Look at your shoes, they're covered in mud.'

'All right, so I did,' Tom shouted. 'And when I do find him I'll take him away from here and never come back. I won't let you put him to sleep, Dad; I won't let you.'

He was sent to his room without any tea, but he knew he'd be called down just as soon as his father had gone out to milk the cows. 'You must be more reasonable,' said his mother. 'Your Dad's only doing what's right. You can't have a sheep-killer for a sheepdog, you know that much.'

'Sam didn't kill the sheep. I told you that, Mum. It was the lion.'

His mother shook her head. 'I just don't understand it when you go on and on with such a ridiculous story.'

'It's true, Mum,' said Tom. His mother shrugged her shoulders. 'Just eat your baked beans, Tom, and let's not talk about it any more.' she said.

That night he waited in bed until he was quite sure everyone in the house was asleep. Within a few minutes he was dressed in all his warm clothes and putting on his boots and coat by the back door. He had Clare's camera around his neck. It was bitter cold outside as he made his way down across the field towards the wood. There was one bright star and a half moon that lit up the night. Once inside the wood he trod carefully, trying not to rustle the leaves. It was a silent night except for the rush of the stream, and a pair of owls calling to each other across the valley.

Tom made his way along the stream to the spot in the wood where he had found Sam the day before. He soon found the perfect place for the meat. On the near side of the stream was a muddy beach and just above it the stump of an old tree. To reach the treestump the lion would have to put a foot in the mud. He left the meat in a pile on the treestump, and sat down behind the trunk of a tree some distance away and waited.

Within half an hour his feet were freezing and he could no longer feel his thumbs; but he stayed there, his camera at the ready. The hours passed and nothing came. He longed to curl up on the ground and go to sleep, but he forced himself to stay awake. All night long he sat there until the first grey light of dawn came up over the moor. Before he left he searched the mud around the treestump for any footprints, but there were none. 'I know you're there. I'm leaving some behind for you,' he called out. 'The rest's for Sam.'

Above him the mountain lion lay in his tree and watched the boy scoop the meat into his coat pocket. He waited until Tom had gone before letting himself down and bounding over to the treestump. He wolfed down the meat and licked the treestump clean.

Tom stayed with Sam in the cottage that morning as long as he could. He watched him eat and then lay down beside him in the hay. He cuddled up close to him to get warm. 'He'll come, Sam. He's got to come. I'm going to spend every night down by that stream till he does. Don't care how long it takes.' He crawled into bed when he got home. That was where his mother found him, fast asleep when she came to wake him. In fact he was so difficult to wake that he almost missed the school bus.

Every day after that Clare brought meat to school and every night Tom put the meat out on the treestump for the lion and waited. One night a family of squabbling badgers ate the lot while Tom looked on, and once a fox came padding across the stream and helped himself. But no lion came, and what's more Tom never found a print in the mud that even looked like the drawing Clare had given him. He began to lose heart. Maybe, he thought, maybe they're right after all. Maybe I imagined everything.

He wasn't to know that every night he spent in the wood he was being watched from the branches high up in the tree above him. He wasn't to know that the lion waited every night till Tom had gone before he came down the tree for his meat. And the lion never put a foot on the mud. He didn't have to.

He leapt from the grass bank on to the treestump with no effort at all.

After a week Tom was tired out. He kept falling asleep in lessons and Mr Morgan told him not to watch television so late. His mother thought he was sickening for something and wanted to keep him away from school. Normally there was nothing that Tom would have liked better. But now Tom needed his supply of lion meat and school was the only place he could get it. He had to go to school.

Clare would be there waiting for him in the playground every morning.

'Any luck?' she'd ask.

'No,' he said. 'Nothing.'

'He'll come,' she would say. 'He's hungry. He'll smell the meat. He'll come. You'll see.' And that was all Tom wanted to hear.

But when he did come at last one cold and windy night Tom was fast asleep. He never heard the lion spring out of his tree. He never heard him come right up to where he lay curled up amongst the leaves. The lion sniffed at the boy's face and then walked away towards the treestump to eat his meat. It was only because a piece of the meat fell into the stream and the lion went splashing in after it that Tom woke. Up until that moment Tom had never been frightened of the idea of meeting the lion. But now he found himself only a few paces from him and he could see just how huge and powerful the creature was, he was suddenly stiff with fear.

The boy and the lion looked at each other for a few moments, and then the lion settled down to his feast again. Tom got to his feet as slowly as he could. He remembered the camera and the picture he had waited all this time to take, but he had only one thought in his head now, to run. He backed away from the lion, never taking his eyes off him, and then turned and ran. He never saw the root that tripped him up. Lights flashed in his head as it hit the side of a treetrunk and then he knew nothing more.

When he woke he felt something heavy pinning him to the ground. He opened his eyes slowly. A giant paw was resting on his chest, and the lion's eyes were peering into his.

# Chapter Five

At first Tom thought he was having a bad dream. Everyone knows the only way to end a bad dream is to wake up. So he tried to wake up and found he couldn't. It was only when the lion began to lick his neck that he was sure it was no dream. The lion's breath was hot on his face and its tongue was exploring the back of his ear. It felt like warm wet sandpaper. Tom closed his eyes and waited to be eaten. At least, he thought, when they find what's left of me they'll know I was telling the truth. They'll know I wasn't making it all up. When the lion began to lick his chin and then his nose, it was more than Tom could stand and he put out a hand and tried to push him away. To his surprise the lion at once stopped licking him and then sat back and yawned.

In the light of the moon Tom noticed something glinting around the lion's neck. He sat up to get a closer look. It was a large silver disc, attached to a broad leather collar, and he could see there were letters on it. Slowly Tom reached out his hand and as he did so the lion rolled on to his back just as Sam did whenever he wanted to be petted. Tom propped himself up on one elbow and began to stroke his tummy. The lion wriggled and squirmed with pleasure as Tom's hand moved up to tickle him under the chin.

'This lion is no man-eater,' Tom thought. 'He likes me.' His fur was thick and warm. Then before Tom knew it two front paws were round his neck and pulling him downwards on top of the lion. Then the licking began all over again. And that was when the lion began to purr, a deep roaring purr. Tom was close enough to read the writing on the disc now. It read *Leo. Tel. Moortown 728.*

Until dawn the boy and the lion wrestled and rolled together amongst the dead leaves. They played by the stream and ran up the hillside onto the moor. By now Tom thought of the lion as no more than a large cat. He could feel the great strength of him but he knew he was quite safe. They liked each other and they trusted each other.

They sat side by side now, looking out across the moor at a rabbit cropping the grass. Suddenly the lion was gone. He leapt the stream and was bounding up the hillside. The startled rabbit bolted into a hole in the hedge and the lion trotted back across the stream, up the mud beach and sat down again to clean his dirty paws.

'Not very good at hunting, are you?' Tom said. 'You're supposed to creep up, not go charging in like the cavalry. But then you're not a wild lion at all, are you? You're just a soppy old pussycat. Well I can't leave you out here, 'cos all you could catch are sheep—and you've had a few of my Dad's already, haven't you? Anyway that name on the collar means you belong to someone, doesn't it?' The lion licked his whiskers, and looked out for more rabbits.

'What am I going to do with you?' said Tom, putting an arm round the lion's neck, 'that's what I'd like to know. If I go back home and tell them you're out here, they won't believe me. And even if they did they'd just hunt you down and shoot you. And I don't want that to happen.'

Tom thought for a moment. 'Only one thing to do. I've got to take you back where you belong. That phone number on your collar should help. We'll go and see Clare. She'll know what to do. She always knows what to do. The problem is, how am I going to get you there? Don't suppose you'll come when you're called like Sam, will you? What I need is a lead.'

He fished around in his coat pocket to see if there was a piece of string in there, but there wasn't. And then he noticed the camera lying in amongst the leaves at the foot of a tree.

'Must have come off my neck when I tripped,' he said. He picked it up and opened the case. 'Be your fault if it's broken.' he said. 'How was I to know you were an old softy. You don't look like it you know.' The camera was not broken, and Tom was just putting it back in its case when he thought of the strap. It was a long one and it was leather, just what he was looking for. 'Don't know if you're trained to go on a lead,' he said, slipping the strap through the lion's collar, 'but we'll soon find out.'

To begin with the lion sat like a rock and looked at him. Nothing Tom did would budge him. He tried sweet-talking him and bribing him with the last of the meat scraps. He tried brute strength, tugging and heaving with all his might.

'Come on, Leo,' he said, 'you got to come. It'll be all right, honest. I won't let them hurt you.' And he pulled again and again, but it was no good. The lion yawned and lay down, head between his paws. But Tom had one more idea to try. 'All right then, if that's how you feel, I'll leave you here, see if I care.' And he dropped the lead and walked away. He had not gone more than fifty yards before he heard the leaves rustling behind him. He turned round to see the lion bounding after him.

'Thought you'd come,' Tom said picking up the lead. 'Don't want to be left alone, do you? Come on now; we got to find Clare, and we haven't got much time. And there's a few people I want you to meet as well. I know you're just a soppy old date, but they don't. I want you to look as fierce as you can. Look hungry, Leo, show them your teeth.' And Tom chuckled at the thought of taking the lion with him into school.

'Course I don't want you to eat them, not even Barry,' he said. 'Don't s'pose he'd taste very nice anyway. I just want you to frighten them, that's all.' And the lion padded along beside him out of the wood and up over the fields towards the town.

Tom's mother went to wake him up at 7 o'clock as usual. His bed was empty. That did not surprise her. Tom often went and made himself a cup of tea if he woke up early. But when she came down to get breakfast ready, she saw the back door was open. That did not surprise her either; Tom's father was always leaving the door open when he went out milking. But as she was closing it she noticed that Tom's boots and coat were not there. She called out around the house. 'Perhaps he's gone off milking with his father,' she thought. So she hurried down the path to the dairy, still in her slippers. Tom wasn't there.

'I'm looking for Tom,' she said.

Tom's father shook his head. 'Hasn't been here,' he said. ''Spect he's off looking for that dog of his. Hardly seen that boy since the dog went off. Give him a shout; he'll be about somewhere.'

'I've been shouting,' said Tom's mother. 'And he hasn't answered. He hasn't come back. He's not here.'

'You think something's wrong, don't you?' Tom's father said.

She nodded. 'I'm worried,' she said. 'He's not been himself ever since Christmas.'

'I'll finish this cow and I'll come,' Tom's father said. 'He'll be about somewhere.'

They searched the farm together, every building and barn, but there was no sign of Tom. They climbed the haystacks and lofts, and ran out across the fields calling for him. They looked along the banks of the stream and combed the wood from end to end.

'Only Ghost Cottage left to check.' said Tom's

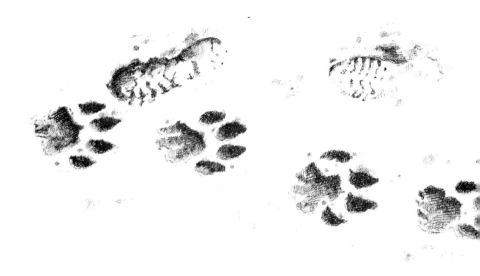

father as they came out of the bottom of the wood. 'If he's not there, then we'll have to call the Police.'

As they came to the door of the cottage they could hear Sam whimpering and whining inside. Tom's father opened the door and the dog bounded out. He tried to catch him, but the dog was past them in a flash and running off into the woods. They followed him shouting for him to come back. But Sam was on the scent of the lion and nothing would stop him. The dog ran as far as the stream, nose to the ground. Once there he sniffed furiously in the leaves. Then his hackles rose and he barked an angry rasping bark. When they caught up with him at last they found the giant footprints in the mud by the stream where Tom had been playing with the lion only an hour or two before. They were too big for a dog, too big for a fox, and too big for a badger. Tom's parents looked at each other. Both of them knew what it was.

'It's Tom's lion, isn't it?' said Tom's mother, crouching down. Tom's footprints were there too. 'And that's Tom's wellington, isn't it?'

'Looks like his size,' said Tom's father. 'And I wouldn't believe him. I wouldn't even listen to him. Now God knows what's happened. I'll never forgive myself, never.'

In the half-light of the early winter morning Tom hurried on towards the town. He knew the countryside like the back of his hand. He crossed roads only when he was sure he wouldn't be seen and stayed well out of sight of the houses and cottages. The lion loped along beside him, and he never once tried to break away.

The town was waking up by the time he got there. Lights were on in the houses everywhere and there were already a few cars out on the roads. Tom sat down with the lion under a hedgerow and wondered how he could get to Clare's house without being seen. 'Can't go up the main street,' he said. 'Too many people about. Can't risk it. We'll have to go round the back. Thing is I've never been round the back of her house. Don't even know if she's got a garden. Still, I know where the shop is and I know she lives there. The butcher's shop is painted pink

45

on the front so it will probably be the same on the back. We'll find it.'

Tom found the house easily enough, for as he crept along the fence behind the houses he saw the butcher's van parked outside. Written on the side he read: 'J. Newman, Butchers of Quality.' The lion smelt the van all over and it was all Tom could do to haul him away. They opened the back gate and ran across the little lawn past a swing and a sandpit to the lighted kitchen window.

Clare was eating her cornflakes at the table and her mother was peering into the toaster by the oven. Tom tapped on the window, but Clare was reading the back of the cornflakes packet and did not even look up. He knocked again, a little louder this time, and Clare's mother turned around. Tom ducked down and held his breath. He heard talking inside. Suddenly the lion was up on his back legs and peering in at the window. Tom tried to pull him down, but he would not come. Then the door opened.

It was Clare who came out, not her mother. She had her glasses in her hand. She looked at the lion, and then put her glasses on and looked at the lion again. 'You found him then? Mum would have had fifty fits if she'd seen that,' she said. The lion hissed at her, and backed away. 'It's all right,' Clare said. 'I won't hurt you. Mum's gone upstairs, Tom. I'm supposed to be watching the toast. I haven't got much time.'

'He's tame,' Tom said. 'Just like a big pussycat, he is.'

'Course he is else you'd be dead, wouldn't you?' she said.

'Thought you said they didn't kill people,' Tom said.

'They don't, except when they've got nothing else to eat,' Clare said. 'What's that thing round his neck?' She came slowly towards the lion, her hand held out. Tom felt the lion stiffen beside him and then relax as Clare crouched down and tickled him behind the ears.

'It's his name, and I think it's a phone number too,' Tom said.

'Leo,' Clare read out. 'That's lion in Latin,' she stood up. 'Soon as I've finished my breakfast and Mum's gone out to work I'll phone up Moortown 728, wherever that is, and I'll tell them to come and fetch him, right?'

'All right,' said Tom, 'but first I'm going to take him to school to show everyone I was telling the truth. And then we'll take him to that rotten Police Station.'

'Then I'll tell them to come and pick him up from the Police Station, shall I?' said Clare. 'Got to go now. You wait in Dad's potting shed at the back of the garden, then we'll go to school together. I want to be there when Barry Parsons sees the lion. Wouldn't miss that for anything.' And she smiled up at Tom, and stroked the lion's head. 'He's beautiful,' she said. 'Isn't he beautiful?' and she turned to go indoors. 'Tom,' she said, 'I think you're very brave, for a boy that is.' And she was gone.

Tom and the lion did not have long to wait in Clare's father's potting shed, but before Clare came for them the lion had overturned almost every pot in the shed. Clare looked at the mess on the floor. 'My Dad won't be very pleased,' she said, shaking her head. 'Never mind, I'll tell him it was a fox. Come on, we'll be late.'

'You phoned up that number?' Tom asked.

'They're coming over right away,' she said. 'The man said he's been missing for over six months now. No one's seen him. They thought he was dead; and it's miles away too, right over the other side of the moor, over sixty miles or more away. He's a long way from home.'

As they came round the corner into the main street, people turned and looked, and then turned and looked again. 'I'm going to enjoy this,' Clare said.

'So am I,' said Tom. 'So am I.'

## Chapter Six

It was five to nine and the playground was full of children when they walked in through the gates with the lion between them. It was rather like dropping a pebble in a pond. As they saw the lion, the children moved slowly backwards to the railings around the playground. One or two ran screaming into the school, but most were quite silent. Tom and Clare stood beside the lion in the middle of the empty playground. A few children whimpered and clung to each other; but most just stared at the lion, paralysed with terror.

Tom looked around the playground until he found who he was looking for. Barry Parsons was standing up against the wall under the conker tree that leaned out over the playground. Tom, Clare and the lion walked slowly towards him. 'He looks terrified,' said Clare.

'Yes he does,' said Tom, 'doesn't he?'

'Don't come any closer,' Barry shouted at them. 'Keep away. He'll kill me.'

'What will?' said Tom.

'That thing, that lion thing. Keep it away.' Barry was swallowing hard. His face had gone quite pale.

'But I thought you said I was making it all up about the lion, Barry,' Tom said. The lion sniffed at Barry's jeans and began to lick them. Barry closed his eyes. 'Looks as if he likes the taste of you, Barry,' said Tom. 'And he hasn't had his breakfast yet.' Barry tried to edge away along the wall. 'Don't try and run away, Barry, else he'll eat you. Just keep quite still.' The lion looked up at Barry and licked his whiskers. Clare tugged at Tom's elbow, and he turned round. Every teacher in the school was gathered in a huddle by the school door, each half-hidden by the other.

''Bye Barry,' said Tom. 'Believe me now do you?' Barry nodded. 'Good,' said Tom. 'Come on Leo, I want you to meet my teacher, Mr Morgan. He didn't believe me either. None of them did.' And they walked across the playground towards the teachers. 'Morning Miss Colvin,' Tom said, trying not to smile. 'Brought something to school to show Mr Morgan.' The teachers gaped. All he could see of Mr Morgan was a white face peering around someone's shoulder. 'Oh he won't hurt. Don't worry, he's quite safe. But he is a lion, isn't he Miss, like I said he was?' Miss Colvin nodded. 'This is the lion I told you I saw Miss. Mr Morgan said I was lying and I wasn't. You said I was lying and I wasn't. So I just brought him to school so as you'd all know I wasn't lying. Clare saw it too Miss. She's not stupid, and she's not a liar either. She can't see very well without her glasses, but she knows a lion when she sees one, and so do I.'

'Now Tom,' said Miss Colvin, unable to take her eyes off the lion. 'I have called the Police. They'll be round any minute. I want you to keep calm Tom. Don't get frightened. Everything will be all right.'

'I'm not frightened, Miss,' said Tom. 'And there's no need for them to come. We're going round to the Police Station now. See Miss, I told them about the lion just like I told you, and they didn't believe me either.'

'I think they'll believe us now,' said Clare.

The main street was empty of people and cars as Tom and Clare and the lion walked out of the school gates and down towards the Police Station. Every door was closed, and every window was full of frightened faces. 'Just like High Noon,' said Clare.

'What's that?' said Tom.

'It's a cowboy film,' said Clare. 'I like black and white cowboy films. There's this Sheriff and the gangsters are coming for him and no one will help him. They all hide in their houses and he's walking down this empty street and then the gangsters come off the train and . . . . . . . .'

'Who wins?' Tom asked.

'The goody of course. They always do in cowboy films.'

As she spoke three Policemen came running down the steps out of the Police Station. One of them was carrying a rifle. They stopped in their tracks as they saw the lion and the two children walking down the road towards them.

'Don't shoot,' Tom called out as one of them dropped to his knee and lifted a rifle slowly to his shoulder. 'Don't shoot, he's just a pet. Won't harm anyone if you leave him alone.'

The three Policemen stared at them. Clare recognised the one with the stripes as the Sergeant who came to give them cycling training at school on Saturday mornings. And both of them knew the one with the rifle. He was the one they had told about the lion, the one who had laughed at them and told them to go away.

'Now don't be frightened, children,' said the Sergeant. 'It'll all be all right if you just keep calm. I want you to do exactly as I say.' He muttered something to the one with the rifle. 'I want you to move away from the lion and walk over to me slowly.'

'They want to shoot him,' Clare whispered. 'They want us out of the way so they can shoot him.' Tom crouched down by the lion and put an arm around his neck.

'No need to shoot him,' Tom said. 'He's as quiet as a mouse. He's just a pet. Wouldn't hurt a fly, would you Leo?'

'You're Tom,' said the Sergeant. 'You're Tom Goss, aren't you?'

'How'd you know that?' Tom asked.

'Your Dad just phoned up,' said the Sergeant. 'Worried sick he was. Said you'd gone missing. He said you might be in danger. Told us there was a lion about. To be honest with you, I didn't believe him, not at first. And then Miss Colvin rings up from the school and says there's a lion in her playground. So I had to believe it then.'

'He didn't believe us either,' said Clare, pointing to the Policeman with the rifle. 'We told him a week ago we'd seen a lion, and he just told us to go away.'

'Did he now?' said the Sergeant. 'You can put that rifle down, Perkins,' he snapped. 'No need for that now.' The rifle was lowered. 'You said he was a pet,' the Sergeant went on. 'Whose pet?'

'I've rung up the people he belongs to,' said Clare. 'Their number's on the lion's collar. They're coming to pick him up, they said. They're on their way now.'

'In that case,' said the Sergeant. 'Why don't we all go inside the Police Station? Perkins here can fetch a bowl of milk for your friend and we can all have a nice cup of tea and I can ring your father and let him know you're all alive and well. How's that?'

And so it was that when Tom's mother and father arrived they found Tom and Clare sitting cross-legged on the floor of the Police Station, and the lion standing with his front feet in a great bowl of milk and lapping noisily. The lion barely looked up as they came in through the door. Tom smiled up at them. 'See?' was all he said.

'We found Sam in the cottage, Tom. Got him in the Land-Rover,' said his father. 'My mistake, Tom. All my mistake.'

'I just didn't want you to shoot him, Dad, that's all,' Tom said. 'Because I knew he didn't do it. He didn't kill your sheep, Dad. In fact he chased Leo away—that's how he got that gash on his leg. You were lucky though. Clare says that cougars can kill fifty sheep in a night if they want to.'

'Cougar? Cougar?' said the Sergeant from behind his desk. 'Perkins, didn't we have a report to keep an eye out for a missing cougar? About nine months ago it must've been. Yes, I know we did. But that's not a cougar is it? That's a mountain lion. I thought a cougar was some kind of an eagle.'

Clare looked up at the Police Sergeant. 'That's a

condor, comes from the Andes mountains in South America,' she said. 'A cougar is a puma, and a puma is a mountain lion. They're all the same. Cougar's a kind of lion. Condor's an eagle.'

'Oh,' said the Sergeant sheepishly.

Another bowl of milk later, a Land-Rover pulled up outside the Police Station. Tom led the lion down the steps and out into the street. The whole town had gathered to watch. There was a line of Policemen holding back the crowds. The newspapers were there and the television cameras.

There was a man in a flat hat standing by the back door of the Land-Rover. 'It was you who found him, was it?' he said, crouching down and running his hand along the lion's back.

'Found him on our farm,' said Tom. 'He's yours, is he?'

'My son's really. 'Bout your age he is. He brought him up since he was a kitten,' said the man. 'Then one day he just took off after a rabbit and didn't come back. We searched and searched for him, but he never came back.'

'He likes rabbits,' said Tom, taking off the lead. ''Bye, Leo,' he said. The lion sprang lightly up into the Land-Rover and then the door shut.

'Thanks a million,' said the man, taking off his cap and shaking Tom by the hand and then Clare. 'How can I ever thank you for what you've done?'

'I think my Dad would like his lambs back,' said Tom. 'Leo got hungry one day and he killed three of my Dad's lambs.'

'Least I can do,' said the man laughing. 'It's a deal.' And he climbed up into his Land-Rover and started the engine. Leo was sitting in the front seat beside him and looking out of the window. He was yawning. As they drove away down the street everyone began clapping and cheering.

Deep in the crowd just outside the Post Office, Uncle Bertie and Aunty Rose stood on tiptoe to try to get a better view. 'That's little Tom, that's my nephew,' said Aunty Rose, tears of pride in her eyes. 'My own nephew. I knew he was telling the truth about that lion. I knew it all the time. I mean you couldn't make up a story like that, could you?'

'No dear,' said Uncle Bertie. 'And he's my nephew too, remember.'

'Oh I could eat him, I could eat that boy I'm so proud of him,' she said.

'Lucky for him the lion didn't feel the same,' said Uncle Bertie, and he laughed and laughed.

'That's not funny,' said Aunty Rose.

'Yes it is,' said Uncle Bertie, and he laughed till he cried.

Back on the steps of the Police Station Tom and Clare stood side by side. 'I feel like the Queen,' said Clare. 'Let's wave back like she does.'

And so they did.